F ... T
CH... ...GH WRITING

First Story changes lives through writing.

There is dignity and power in telling our own story. We help disadvantaged young people find their voices.

First Story places professional writers into secondary schools serving low-income communities, where they work intensively with students and teachers to foster confidence, creativity and writing ability.

Our programmes expand young people's horizons and raise aspirations. Students gain vital skills that underpin their success in school and support their transition to further education and employment.

To find out more and get involved, go to www.firststory.org.uk.

First published 2019 by First Story Limited
Omnibus Business Centre, 39–41 North Road, London, N7 9DP

www.firststory.org.uk

ISBN 978-0-85748-389-8

1 3 5 7 9 10 8 6 4 2

A CIP catalogue record for this book is available from the British Library.

Printed and bound in the UK by Aquatint
Typeset by Avon DataSet Ltd
Copyedited by Gemma Harris
Proofread by Beth Kruszynskyj
Cover illustration and design by Rebecca Gibbon www.rebeccagibbon.com

Our Story, Their Story, Every Story

A collection of extra ordinary people

An Anthology by the First Story Group
at Lawn Manor Academy

EDITED BY REBECCA TANTONY | 2019

FIRST STORY
CHANGING LIVES THROUGH WRITING

As Patron of First Story I am delighted that it continues to foster and inspire the creativity and talent of young people in secondary schools serving low-income communities.

I firmly believe that nurturing a passion for reading and writing is vital to the health of our country. I am therefore greatly encouraged to know that young people in this school – and across the country – have been meeting each week throughout the year in order to write together.

I send my warmest congratulations to everybody who is published in this anthology.

Camilla

HRH The Duchess of Cornwall

Contents

Introduction

Rebecca Tantony, Writer-in-Residence

When I was fourteen years old, I had no idea what I wanted to be. Most of my school years were spent with a fluttering heart and the want to run as far as possible from the classroom. I do know that if someone had told me my story was worth hearing – and the more I shared it, the more I would make sense of who I was – I would have listened to them. These students remind me of all the words I wanted to say, but just didn't know how to.

Together, through the avenue of language, we have examined and explored, mourned and celebrated; we have written six-word stories, recipes for loved ones, poems around the themes of belonging and home, politics, identity and the self. Some stories spoke of memories from childhood and future dreams yet to be captured. The students showed up week by week and brought themselves fully into that classroom. They are hilarious and clever, always engaged and open to try new ideas, always willing to share themselves with expression and sincerity.

It has been incredible to have the amazing poet Saili Katebe along on the journey with us, contributing his wisdom, insight and ideas. He brought an invaluable dynamic into the space. I am beyond grateful to him.

On the recent drive from Bristol to Swindon, ecstatic at the thought of another workshop with these students, I had a pang of sadness, knowing the project would be finished soon. Moments later the same pang turned into an overwhelming joy, a party popper set off in my heart, at the thought of these stories being celebrated around kitchen tables, on bus journeys, through the eyes and ears of both family and strangers. I trust, through the ordinary and everyday actions of their lives, that these young people will go on to be the next generation of change-makers in this world. They are passionate, caring and able to see what humanity needs to flourish. And I hope they keep telling the story of who they are for ever. Starting with the pages of this anthology, with humour, honesty and hope, then next in their educations, jobs, lives ahead. Theirs are stories that deserve to be heard.

Teacher's Foreword

Jayne Rafferty, English Teacher

About eight months ago, I met with eighteen young people, stared them dead in the eyes and informed them, in all seriousness, that they would be published writers within the year.

It was a bold claim and I'm not sure they really believed me. Teachers are known for putting a positive spin on things, so I couldn't blame the group of students I was talking to for eyeing me dubiously. Their polite smiles somehow managed to be both sympathetic and mistrustful at the same time. *Sure, Miss*, those smiles seemed to say. *Sure we will.* However, this book is the proof that it isn't always a line.

When I started searching for students to approach for the First Story project, I was looking for something that is hard to put into words. We'll call it The Spark. The Spark is elusive and tricky and no one really knows what it is, but we all know it when we read it. It's something in a person's writing that makes us sit up straighter, pay attention, get excited. It's not necessarily about punctuation or spelling or grammar, although those things can help. It's more than that. It's the ability to take something as obvious and commonplace as words, something we use every day in shopping lists and texts and conversations about what to have for tea, and then use them to make something new. People with The Spark take words and turn them into something wonderful. All of the students whose work you'll read in this book have The Spark. They had it when we started, and they still have it now. But now, I hope that they *know* they have it, and that they are as proud of it as they should be. The work you'll read in this anthology is something truly special. Some of it is fiercely, savagely funny. Some of it is deliciously surreal. Some of it is angry and raw. Some of it is shockingly, powerfully moving. All of it is important.

Over our sessions, with the talented Rebecca and Saili guiding us, we have explored types of writing that we didn't know existed. We've learned how something as seemingly insignificant as words can shed a light that helps us to see things about the world, and about ourselves, that maybe we weren't aware of before. I've been lucky enough to read some truly incredible writing during this project; some amazingly perceptive thoughts, expressed in endlessly original ways. Every student involved has thrown themselves into the challenges of the project with a determination that has left me in awe. I am prouder of them than I can say.

I've enjoyed every moment of the process of creating this anthology. I hope the students have too. I'm sure you'll agree that this finished product is something rare and precious. Please enjoy it. And, I'll let you in on a secret: everyone has The Spark. Most people don't realise it, but it's there all the same. You have it. For you, it might not be writing. Maybe your Spark is in Art or Drama or Music or Maths. All you need to do is find it and let it burn bright.

A Recipe of Me

Ryan Andrews

5 shots of espresso

3 tablespoons of sugar

50 litres of Coca-Cola

1 salad of your choice

5 slices of pepperoni pizza

Bake until burnt

The Girl in the Photograph

Holly Jones

She looks up to me and smiles, as if to say,

I knew it.

I knew that you would be gone from me and I would turn into
you. It's true.
She's just like me. She makes me.
The grass swaying in her eyes as she concentrates.
Her eyebrows are different from mine but

still originate in the same place. Our genes.
Her cheeky grin in her photos has turned to my hard stare.
It's a grow-up, a glow-up, a realisation.
A nation,
a clarification,

of who she was and who I am. She's changed,
somehow.

Was it being picked up? Was it fighting?
Was it heartbreak?

Was it life in general?
Who knows?

I know.

I know her smile, her talent and her temper tantrums.
I know my smile, my talent and my temper tantrums.
        I know her because I know
myself.

Who Am I?

Ellie-Tess Webb

My name smells like tea,
sounds like my mum's name,
tastes like Snickers.
My nickname is Els Bels.
My name looks like graffiti
on an abandoned wall.

Win

Denzil Miranda

One hot, sunny, warm afternoon, I was sweating waterfalls. Bored and I didn't know what to do.

I remembered I had leftover Christmas money, so I went to check it. I was surprised to find £60, so I decided to go to GAME and try to buy something.

Walking down the corridor, suddenly, in the corner of my eye, I saw a game that looked really interesting. Unexpectedly, a blue light came out of me, which directly linked with the game.

Quickly, and out of nowhere, I was in the game's perspective. All of the games around started disappearing like a time-lapse.

After approximately thirty seconds, I saw someone who looked exactly like me. Who had every single detail that I had. I realised it was me.

The link disconnected and I was in my own body. I felt I had to buy this game, like it was some treasure that I had to acquire.

I went home and played the game and the very first game I played, I got a Victory Royale. From that day on, my life changed. I got famous, I legally changed my name to Game, I had a zoo in my backyard, I got so, so rich I invented a cure for death, all down to that one game.

That's a win for my life.

Tops and Bottoms

Beate Eversone

I come from sweet, sparkling champagne and ugly natural
disasters.
I'm from the biggest regrets and the most interesting
Hollywood films.
I come from big and grey smoke clouds and toys from childhood.
I'm from fire and Hybrid, okay with sun.

I come from treetops and all imaginary animals. I'm from
rude nightmares
but in my heart I'm a big, fluffy, innocent teddy who does not
sit in the corner
but goes to Starbucks with besties to drink some iced coffee.
True fact: I am a baby who made her own life, made her own
decisions.

In the End

Sristi Gurung

It's black and dark,
like the locked-up rooms shunned out from society.
It's a grey thunderstorm that people hate
yet somehow I feel comfort
in the pouring rain.

A proud, shining electric guitar with broken strings
now forgotten in the depths.
It's not yellow like the sun that seeps through the blinds.
It's not bright and warm like holding hot tea in the winter.
It's cold and dark
like the locked-up rooms shunned out from society.

Mirage

Krisha Gurung

Happiness is all around us.
Sometimes we see it but sometimes we miss it.
If I don't have it, I blame myself for my misfortune.
I'm stuck in this swamp, struggling under the scrutinising glare of the association we call Society.
Slowly

Sinking.
A habit of comparing myself to others, expectations high so I can disappoint badly,
the path of my unseen future blurry and carved out in mismatched pieces.
My mother's dream of conception, wrecked by the feeble me.
What was supposed to be a memory, is now an old fisherman's tale.

Sparks Fly

Charlie Starkey

It was a dark, cold and foggy night; there was a distinct smell of freshly lit bonfire in the air.

We warned my dad, whilst lighting the firework, as the harsh winter winds were starting to pick up.

But it was too late.

At the speed of light, the bright orange flame shot off into our neighbour's shed. The vibrant colours of blue, red and green flared around us.

With a very faint siren in the background, we found ourselves inside, waiting for our punishment. And ever since that day we have never lit a firework.

2017

Deren Oktar

I remember setting firecrackers off at 6 a.m.
It was sweet revenge.
One evening, on holiday, we were sitting under the canopy,
playing our card games, eating, and drinking juice.
It was a chill evening.

We don't like the neighbouring kids.
Never have, never will.
They thought it would be a fantastic idea to get us
wet with a large hosepipe.

But the next morning, we wanted to have a little fun…
Sadly, this just happened to be the morning I had to leave.
So my friends set off some firecrackers and
I do not know what happened next. I was gone.

Stay Still

Maria Lisboa

He was like a white, empty canvas, given to a lazy artist.
No colour or emotion could be seen.
He was similar to the cat from the Chinese zodiac sign –
unwanted, uninvited and completely useless.
He stood still, glaring at me with his cold, harsh stare.
There was a slight hint of loneliness in the air between us.
It seemed as if we were two magnets of the same pole,
we repelled, got more distant.
He was like a traffic light,
he had the deep desire for everything to stop,
Waiting until that button was finally pushed.
Every moment I was with him,
I was reminded of a piano song.
Sad yet glorious melodies played through my head non-stop.
I was reminded of the ocean.
A beautiful blue.
The waves leaving things behind on the sand:
Needles, razors, knives, saws.
And, sadly, cold words to hurt me.

But I never listened.

Those eyes that warned me not to get close,
otherwise you would
throw another tantrum.

Even though you do those things,
Why do you stay still and not run away from me?

Why is that?
Why do you stay still?

Dear friend
Try to be happier.
Don't keep your eyes the same shade of blue.
The colour of the cold winter winds, blowing me away from you.

Always in My Heart

Samina Omar

She's my only happiness. My love and everything. The day she left broke me.
I am missing her more with every day that passes.

Tears most nights,
but knowing I have to get used to it. It will take time.

Her cheeky-cheese smile and her bubbly, funny laugh. Her happiness.
What she had with us will be in my memories for ever.

Holding her hand through all those forgotten times.

KFC, My Wife, the Love of My Life

Joey Godwin

I remember the day I saw the vibrant flash of red.
My eyes glued to the building as I passed by.
Mouth open wide with dribble falling out.
There was a glow, shining on the giant structure.

It was then I knew that she,

the crumbly, thick, mouth-watering chicken, was the one.

But time has now passed, grumbling stomach, more food.
The dreadful day came –
the death of my wife, the love of my life.

RIP. KFC.

Bitterness

John Wetton

I taste bitter,
I taste sour.
I feel juices that run through me,
I smell soap from hands,
The steel from knives,
I hear chops as blades part me,
I am in agonising pain.
I see the world before I die. What am I?

A Diary

Maria Lisboa

I can only see the darkness from the angle I was dropped.
As I cautiously turn around, I notice that she is not there.
I wonder what must have made her upset throughout these
 days.
I smell tears on top of me,
I touch the words written all over my body.
The taste of many letters made me happy,
until a few mean comments got in the way.
The number of insulting comments started to increase,
 bit by bit.
I look back at where she would have been and she is silently
 sitting there.
In her right hand she is holding a few pills.
In her left hand, she is holding a knife.
She is so indecisive.
I go back to reading the words on my snow-white skin.
One word makes me worry.
Suicide.
I look back at the girl,
she has now left this world –

Over-Large Hoodie

Samina Omar

It's black and no, it ain't no bright colours.
It's the upsetting piano all alone.
It's no happy melody played though fingers, no.

The emotion of the rain pouring down.

The over-large hoodie which makes me at home.

And the words broken though my heart.
It's no sunny day. It's no fancy sparkling dress.

The One Who Made Her Do It

Ella Drake

You walk home alone, worrying that someone is following you. Well, in Sharon's case someone was: her bully Helen. Helen and her gang, yelling, 'You're a bitch!' She got rinsed, she was mourning. She ran into her house and leapt up the stairs.

Her mum shouted, 'Are you alright, hon?'

She replied, 'Yeah.'

After two hours had passed, her mother and father left.

'Bye hon, we'll be back in three hours. We've left dinner in the fridge. Love you.'

Sharon replied, 'Love you too.'

She watched them leave.

As soon as they did, she went into her pencil case. She got her scissors and she started cutting her arm. She thought about getting a knife. She went downstairs to get one, but then there was a knock at the door and it was Helen. Sharon slammed the door and locked it, then ran upstairs to see if Helen was still there. Gone.

The next day came along. She was getting ready, then received a text from an unknown number. She opened it.

I am gonna get u at school. C u there, BITCH!!

She ignored it, got her bag and left.

But Helen was waiting for her at the gate with her gang. Sharon tried to walk past them, but they pulled her by the arm.

'I told you I was gonna get you when you got to school.'

'We aren't in school yet, so get off me.' She wanted to stay inside, but there was nothing but silence.

Helen smacked her round the face and pulled her hair. Sharon cried. Helen's gang laughed and started kicking her on the floor. They all spat on her. One by one, they walked off laughing. Sharon was a wound that didn't stop bleeding. She got up and walked into school.

Sharon ran home.

Her mum said, 'Hon, what happened?'

Sharon lied.

'Nothing. I'm fine.'

'You don't look it, and why are you home early?'

'I AM FINE AND I GOT SENT HOME! JEEZ, LEAVE ME ALONE!'

So she left her alone.

Later, Sharon's mum called up the stairs. No reply.

She walked up saying, 'Sharon, this isn't funny. Your dinner's getting cold.'

When she saw, she broke into tears, knelt next to her daughter's body. Sharon's father came running upstairs, knelt beside his wife.

Sharon's funeral came and Helen was there with her gang behind a tree.

One of Helen's friends said, 'We went too far.'

A rose on the grave.

A tear dropped onto the coffin.

A BELOVED DAUGHTER gone.

Pressure

Sam Ball Blackmore

It is red.
A guitar on a cold night doing a solo,
it will never be warm until it's over.
It is just turned on and then,
forgotten about.
It's a heavy thing that weighs you down.

It's not a bright yellow that everyone likes.
It's not a drum in a band that makes people happy.
It's not sunny and warm.
It's not a new, shiny top that you just bought.
You will never escape from it.

Shadows

Sahira Xec

Excessive amounts of colours, people, personalities,
and yet I still can't speak. Why?
Peel off the skin and throw it away.
What do you have left? Bones that hold you up, but not for this.
Curiosity killed the cat.
Close yet far, different but the same.
The epitome of life.
Towering above us, casting an overpowering shadow,
Those who know it will feel it.
'What are you? Who are you?'
Numerous questions, no answers,
Bystanders surround the scene.
It makes us diverse, original and interesting.
So why am I stuck in this everlasting spiral of darkness?

The Weapon of Depression Cuts Deep Like a Blade

Samina Omar

Innocent hearts destroyed. Isolated people, risking their lives. Upset families, stressed and depressed.

Broken, hurt and crying yourself to sleep. Mad slits on wrists. 'Hope' is all you can ask for.

Keep, trust and believe in yourself. You can overcome this fear.

The Darkest Relations

Holly Jones

It is the colour yellow.

It is not a harp played adjacent to a beautiful orchestra.
It is a well-worn hoodie covering the joy.
It is not sunny, it is cloudy.
It tells me to look,

Look for me, it tells me.

It sings this to a piano, played by the deepest mellow pianist.
Unfortunately,
It is not a delicate white dress, worn on a breezy summer's day.

No,
It is the duvet I curl up in that says *you will never be alone.*

My Thoughts

Beate Eversone

I was sitting in the lap of my human. I thought, *Yeah, yeah, we are happy*. Would I still be the no one in the corner, if she hadn't found me? Would I be lost, sitting in pain and looking for food? But at the end she came, she rescued me. Everything is how I imagined it would be. Everything is purrrrrfect.

Soft, White and Fluffy

Maria Lisboa

I remember its soft, white fur.
It was the bunny my dad had rescued.
I remember feeling happy yet curious.

My old house –
the walls were painted white,
the living room decorated with different pieces of furniture.
I remember hearing my mother scream.
I knew what had happened in her past.
A bunny bit her and after that she could no longer think they were innocent.
In my memory,
I can smell mud.
I can see that the bunny,
such a small and fragile creature,
wanted my help.
It looked so miserable.
My mum made my dad return the poor little creature to where it came from,
A few days later we received news that it had died.

Blood is an Acronym

John Wetton

Blood dripping down his head,
past his eyes, down his face.
The sill that makes him trip,
nails and tacks, pulled from the carpet,
small steps seem to never end,
playing and hiding, getting in trouble.
He catches his foot,
goes into the tacks,
black and blue, cuts and
bruises. Lethal wounds,
leaking liquid. Oxygenated
cells, transportation. Oozing
red, filled with steel.
Dripping down, scabbing
over. He's lucky he lives.
Blood dripping on his hand,
tears running down his chin,
fixed, but forever scarred.

War

John Wetton

Sound of silence, loud bangs,
Blood dripping down my arm. People falling.
Guns are firing.
I am going,
We have lost.

Homework

Charlie Wright

It is red.
It is not a violin because that is soothing.
It is a drum being bashed violently.
It is not a scorching sun during a heatwave.
It is a thunderstorm thrashing and crashing.
It is not shorts, filling people with freedom,
It is a hoodie on the darkest of days.
It says it's useless.
It says it isn't good at anything.
It is… homework.

The Pen Talks

Kray Wyatt

I can taste the feeling of a stressful moment,
I can feel the relationship with limited time.
I can smell the thickness of paper,
I can hear the silence of concentration,
I can see the look of frustration.

Socks

Sahira Xec

The colour yellow, like the one on my report card.
A sad, broken violin, only able to play so much until another
  string snaps.
Overpowering grey clouds above our heads;
It takes a drop of rain to know what we need: umbrellas.
Cold, wet pairs of socks that nobody wants to wear.
'Hurry up and stop wasting time!'
It's not like a soft pink or a piano solo in an empty room.
Nothing close to the sun seeping in through the clouds.
It's not a pair of shoes that protect your feet from the icy,
  damp floor,
And that's why your socks are dripping.

Powerful Creation

Denzil Miranda

I taste electrical instruments of power.
I feel letters and numbers getting input
at the speed of 500,000 words per hour.
I see the electrical pulses flow,
I hear the keyboard getting thrown,
I smell the choke and charge burning.
I am the most powerful creation living.

Wasted

Charlie Starkey

My childhood was wasted,
the opportunities I could have tasted.

I could've been taught how to fill in an application,
instead I learnt abstract equations.

Didn't get taught how to pay tax,
instead they devoted time to Shakespeare's classics.

They beat my creativity,
Made me think intellectually,

There was stuff they weren't telling me,
It made me lose my vitality.

The Window Talks

Sam Ball Blackmore

I taste many hands opening me on a summer's day.
I feel the strong wind coming through.
I smell the fresh air when they open me.
I hear a mix between people talking,
then a tranquil and beautiful silence.

I Remember When

Kray Wyatt

I remember when I had my first Christmas with a decent
amount of snow.
I could see the whitest of skies and smell the cold air entering
my body
when I breathed. I was full of happiness and joy. I could hear
the laughter
of my family, whilst we gradually built an army of snowmen.

The Apartment

Sahira Xec

I taste their feet going through.
Hard, heavy steps each time.
All I ever smell is the pollution, smoke and petrol,
McDonald's from across the street.
Looming above everything, I see tiny dots,
sporadically placed around me.
I hear laughter and happy conversations.
Why can't I ever be like them?
I touch the hues of blue above
and the earth below.

Pablo Geckobar

Deren Oktar

Inside the box lies a minuscule gecko. On Christmas Day, Rebecca jumps down her staircase to be greeted by a box. Herb. Herb is on holiday, by himself, from Mexico. Back in his hometown, he is known as Pablo. He has two beautiful wives and one hard-working child. He owns nine Aston Martins and 334 Bentleys. *How does he have all of this?*

A Note to Self

Ryan Andrews

1) Try not to get scammed out of ***your*** happiness and opinions.

2) Believe in ***yourself*** more than you believe in anyone else.

3) Don't give up just because others already have.

4) Opinions are not facts.

5) Your family cares most.

My First Roller-Coaster Experience

Joey Godwin

I feel the ups

and downs,
the turn arounds.
I taste the air filling my mouth.

I smell the sweat of adrenalin.

I hear the rush of the leaves,
the screaming people. I see the start

and then we come to a stop.

The End of Spring

Sristi Gurung

As spring comes to an end,
a wave of melancholy washes over me.
Without regret, the cherry blossoms start to fall and scatter.
Our meeting was short but it was real.
Even though this cannot last
I won't resent it, because nothing is for ever.
The gentle breeze stirs the jade chimes
As I stare at the moon, high above the cherry blossom tree,
troubled by countless unanswered questions.

The Song of Happiness

Denzil Miranda

I remember, remember,
when Big Shaq released a song that was great.
That day the memes were the best.
I remember, remember,
I listened as I lay in my bed.
I remember, remember,
that cold and sad day,
and the song which made my heart sway.

The Planet

Ellie-Tess Webb

I come from my family's warm heart, that we all share,
from my nan's welcoming cups of milky tea, which never had biscuits to spare.
From my dad's duct-taped boxing bag with holes everywhere,
from *Dora the Explorer*, who I will never leave behind,
from my uncle's oversized hoodies.
The lakes at Coate Water, where long walks with my friends took place,
Where memories were made.
I come from the stairs by the big, green gates, that grew small as we grew tall,
I come from my dog's loving paws, which are now lost in the stars.
From the long line of books which fill boxes to the brim.
I come from a single planet in the universe.

Untitled

Krisha Gurung

Childhood.
A beautiful cinematography,
filled with wondrous minds and the colour white.

Here I am trying to return to the pretend world of Neverland,
a place which no longer exists but I can't let go of.
I am unfamiliar with the act of closure, the idea too
frightening.
My lifelong obstacles sugar-coated into peaceful mountains, all
an illusion of dreams.
The connected chains of reality pull me back, and the colour
white slowly slips away.

Life Story

Beate Eversone

Do you remember when, as a child, you always wanted to be a ballerina? Well yeah, that was me. In nursery, I would always dream that I was dancing. There would only be one image in my head: white tutus, floor-length mirrors.

Through years, my mind changed from ballerina to doctor, from that to zookeeper, and then finally I came to songwriter and actor. My mum moved away to the UK without me, and for a few years I was travelling from Latvia to visit her. And then (ha ha) came my four siblings. And OMG, they're so cute. That's it about them.

I'm thirteen now and I realise that I wanted to change something. Everyone said that a healthy lifestyle could help. And you know what? It does, so try it. If you're reading this then my advice is to always remember: no matter what, just don't give up. Fight for it. I once gave up on my exercise, gave up on the dream of movement. And now I have found it again, I will never stop dancing.

A Look Back to the Future

Holly Jones

Your talent shines through your chubby cheeks,
it glows through your atrocious self-cut hair.
You will grow to care. You may run off in a strop and cry the roof off,

but, you will change.

You shouldn't have cut your hair.

Your parents wouldn't have banned you from everything if you hadn't. Remember that one.
You will regret it in the future. However, I loved you.
I grew into a teenager;

you'll know. You will too.

Biographies

Ryan Andrews: His name is Ryan Andrews but he prefers Ryan Christopher. His hobbies are go-karting, travelling and gaming. He has a Maisie (dog). He has a few mates. He has a family. His favourite foods are his mum's pork balls and noodles. His dream is to go to Thailand.

Sam Ball Blackmore: Sam is thirteen years old and his favourite takeaway food is KFC. His favourite sport is football and his favourite football team is Liverpool FC. Sam also likes to play PS4 with his friend.

Ella Drake: Ella is thirteen years old, soon to be fourteen. She is lactose intolerant, which means she can't eat or drink milk or anything that contains milk. The things she loves are her family, friends and food. The things she hates are bullying and homework. She hopes you enjoy her story.

Beate Eversone: Hey, she's Beate! She's from Latvia – Riga, to be exact. Latvia is a really small country but there are really nice people. If you don't know where Latvia is, it is next to Russia. Before Beate came to the UK she didn't know what she wanted to do when she grew up. But now she knows that she wants to be a singer. Her gran says she's the biggest drama queen ever but Mum wants her to dance. You know what? She'll make a song about dancing drama.

Joey Godwin: Joey loves all things to do with sport, mainly boxing and basketball. He aspires to be a boxer one day, and an artist in his spare time. P.S. He can flip his eyelids and loves to have fun, like parties.

Holly Jones: Holly is fourteen and a half. She likes long car journeys and watching the rain (without touching it). She also would like to travel the world, starting with Greece and ending with Rome. She thinks outside the circle.

Maria Do Carmo Martins Lisboa: Maria Do Carmo Martins Lisboa is thirteen years old. Her name means 'garden of flowers' and her favourite flower is a dandelion. Her favourite subject is geography, but she would like her future profession to be Spanish teacher. She enjoys watching anime; her favourite is *Tokyo Ghoul*. She would describe herself most as 'Heroine' from *Amnesia*, since they are both serious and despise getting into trouble. If she had to choose, her favourite cuisine would be Mexican and she would say that she's a realist-optimist.

Sristi Gurung: Sristi Gurung was born in Hong Kong and came to the UK two years later. She would like to be a vet and her favourite lesson is computing. Her least favourite is Spanish. One of her most enjoyed series is *2 Moons*, which is an LGBT Thai series. Her favourite colours are black, grey and white. She likes the character Kou Yukina and her favourite food is hotpot. Her friends describe her as a reserved person who gets competitive when it comes to sports, especially basketball. She dislikes waking up early in the morning and walking around in the hot, humid weather. However, she likes reading and watching horror and is a fan of the manga artist Junji Ito.

Denzil Miranda: Denzil's favourite colour is blue. He is from India, Goa to be exact. His favourite movie is *Johnny English*. He is small but with a big heart. His best quality is his humour; he makes everyone laugh. His best memory is when he got his pup on his birthday. His hobby, normally, is to play games.

DEREN OKTAR: He is special. He likes food, but still doesn't eat much. No friends. Okay, that's a lie. He loves to travel and has a house.

SAMINA OMAR: Samina is fourteen years old, and she would love to go all around the world and travel to different places. She is funny, annoying, and beautiful, and always knows how to cheer people up. No matter what, she is always there for family and real friends, who are always in her heart.

CHARLIE STARKEY: His favourite colour is green. He is very sarcastic, however, he is liked by most people. His favourite memory is when he went to Weymouth with his family, and he lives without regrets. He wishes he could live his life for fun and enjoy it.

ELLIE-TESS WEBB: Ellie-Tess Webb converts oxygen into carbon dioxide.

KRISHA GURUNG: Krisha was born in the month of February, the shortest month of the Julian and Gregorian calendars, in southern Kowloon, Hong Kong. She enjoys spending time with her friends and listening to music. Her favourite subject is history and she is the weakest in maths. In the future, she would like to visit her home country Nepal again.

JOHN WETTON: John is fourteen years old. He likes bad jokes and he loves to eat. He has a talent for chess and he can shake his eyes. He loves to cook and he wants to be a chef.

CHARLIE WRIGHT: Charlie is thirteen. He likes gaming and eating. He's mentally seventy-seven, physically thirteen and virtually six. He's from Swindon but wants to live in Dubai. He has a dog called Amber and two cats called Rosie and Ging. He wants to be a comedian or something.

Kray Wyatt: Kray is thirteen years old. Kray's favourite thing is technology. His favourite activity is playing the PS4 and his most enjoyed food is a roast dinner. But don't get him wrong! He also favours a good, old fashioned takeaway.

Sahira Xec: Sahira is fourteen. She is always ready to watch Netflix or talk to her friends. She can be described as the colour mint-green since she is chilled and relaxed. Despite this, she can relate to Chandler from *Friends* as they both use humour as a 'coping mechanism' and choose sarcasm, accompanied by a relentless number of awkward jokes, as their form of irony. Her favourite TV shows are both *Friends* and *Brooklyn 99*. She is a realist-pessimist and her personality type is ENFP.

Acknowledgements

Melanie Curtis at Avon DataSet for her overwhelming support for First Story and for giving her time in typesetting this anthology.

Gemma Harris for copy-editing this anthology and supporting the project.

Rebecca Gibbon for illustrating and designing the cover of this anthology.

David Greenwood and Foysal Ali at Aquatint for printing this anthology at a discounted rate.

The Dulverton Trust who supported First Story in this school.

HRH The Duchess of Cornwall, Patron of First Story.

Thanks to:
Arts Council England, Alice Jolly & Stephen Kinsella, Andrea Minton Beddoes & Simon Gray, The Arvon Foundation, BBC Children in Need, Beth & Michele Colocci, Blackwells, Boots Charitable Trust, Brunswick, Charlotte Hogg, Cheltenham Festivals, Clifford Chance, Dulverton Trust, Edith Murphy Foundation, First Editions Club Members, First Story Events Committee, Frontier Economics, Give A Book, Ink@84, Ivana Catovic of Modern Logophilia, Jane & Peter Aitken, John Lyon's Charity, John Thaw Foundation, Miles Trust for the Putney & Roehampton Community, Old Possum's Practical Trust, Open Gate Trust, Oxford University Press, Psycle Interactive, Royal Society of Literature, Sigrid Rausing Trust, The Stonegarth Fund, Teach First, Tim Bevan & Amy Gadney, Walcot Foundation,

Whitaker Charitable Trust, William Shelton Education Charity, XL Catlin, our group of regular donors, and all those donors who have chosen to remain anonymous.

Most importantly we would like to thank the students, teachers and writers who have worked so hard to make First Story a success this year, as well as the many individuals and organisations (including those who we may have omitted to name) who have given their generous time, support and advice.